T0195974

Berty Bat

and The

Poorly Witch

AUDREY BROWN

AuthorHouse™ UK
1663 Liberty Drive
Bloomington, IN 47403 USA
www.authorhouse.co.uk
UK TFN: 0800 0148641 (Toll Free inside the UK)
UK Local: 02036 956322 (+44 20 3695 6322 from outside the UK)

Because of the dynamic nature of the Internet, any web addresses or links contained
in this book may have changed since publication and may no longer be valid. The views
expressed in this work are solely those of the author and do not necessarily reflect the
views of the publisher, and the publisher hereby disclaims any responsibility for them.

This book is printed on acid-free paper.

ISBN: 978-1-6655-9821-7 (sc)
ISBN: 978-1-6655-9822-4 (e)

Print information available on the last page.

Published by AuthorHouse 04/19/2022

Berty Bat
and The
Poorly Witch

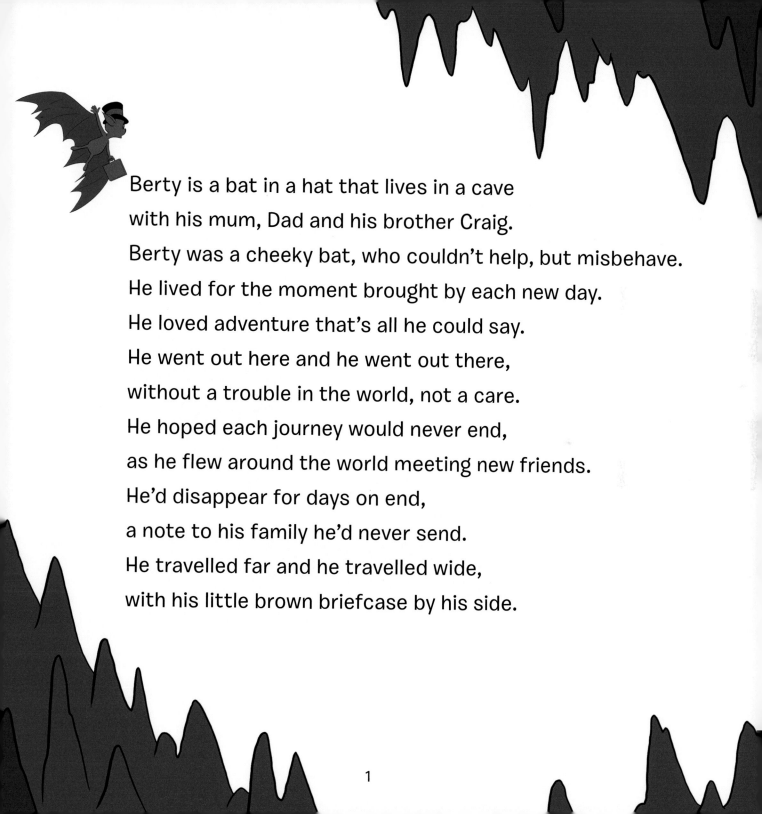

Berty is a bat in a hat that lives in a cave

with his mum, Dad and his brother Craig.

Berty was a cheeky bat, who couldn't help, but misbehave.

He lived for the moment brought by each new day.

He loved adventure that's all he could say.

He went out here and he went out there,

without a trouble in the world, not a care.

He hoped each journey would never end,

as he flew around the world meeting new friends.

He'd disappear for days on end,

a note to his family he'd never send.

He travelled far and he travelled wide,

with his little brown briefcase by his side.

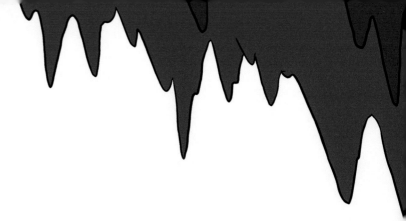

One day as Berty travelled around,

he heard really a rather a strange sound.

A bit of a cackle, or a witchy cry,

a disturbing sound, not a time to act shy.

Berty swooped through the air and down to a shed.

Berty peered through the window, a witch was in bed.

She didn't look well, though witches never do!

She was laid on her bed sneezing, "Achoo!"

The witch kept coughing and looked very hot;

her nose was dripping with slimy green snot.

"Achoo!" sneezed the witch and made Berty jump,

he flapped his wings hard, and the window went 'Bump!'

"What are you doing?" screamed the witch reaching for her wand,

but when she began to wave it, Berty was gone.

All that remained was a hat, tiny and small,

the witch picked it up and with a wave of her wand, there was no hat at all.

Berty was hiding under the ledge,

but Berty's hat was gone and he made a pledge...

"I will get my hat back whatever it takes,

taking my hat, that witch has made a mistake."

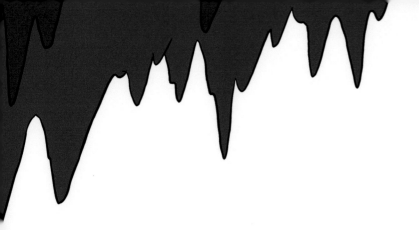

Berty swooped back to the window and knocked on it hard,

"You've lost my hat witch, and it's not rubbish to discard."

The witch started laughing and picked up her wand,

"Get off my window, bat be gone."

Berty cried, "Please don't hurt me,"

"I wanted to help you," he started to plea.

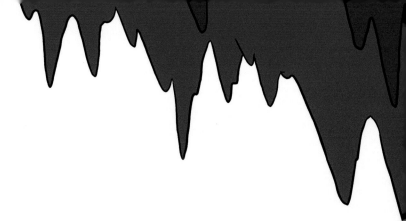

The witch looked startled and she lowered her wand,
"You wanted to help me all along?"
"Yes" announced Berty "You seem very ill,
that's why I perched on your windowsill."
The witch full of wonder replied, "But I am a witch whom nobody likes."

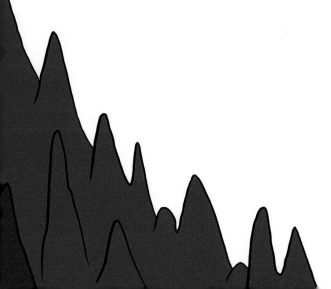

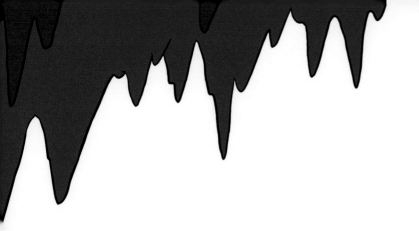

I live with my fleas, ticks, spiders and mites.

I make cakes from slugs and snails,

and do spells using worms and old fingernails."

"Yes," said Berty. "You don't sound very well.

I thought that you may need a friend to get you through

this poorly spell?"

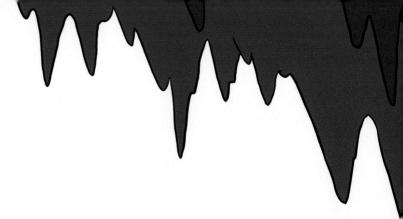

The witch cackled loud "Witches don't need or have friends,
though this sneezing is driving me around the bend."
Berty asked "May I come in?"
"Ok," said the witch with a very big grin.
A witch's grin is a sight for sore eyes,
but Berty smiled back and flew inside.
Berty made the witch some soup and fluffed up her pillows,
"Thank you," said the witch "You are a kind little fellow."

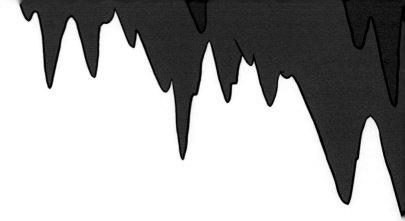

Berty and the witch played games for hours on end,

they played hide and seek and let's pretend.

"I must go home now," said Berty, "My family will be worried."

He gathered his briefcase in a bit of a hurry.

"Thank you for having me it's been great,

but I must get home now, it's getting late."

"Thank you for helping me", replied the witch,
and with that she gave her wand a little twitch.
With a bit of a 'bang' and a 'flash' of red,
Berty's hat was back on his head.
They smiled at one another and said "Goodbye";
Berty flapped his wings and took to the sky.

Berty arrived home with a story to tell,
of how he made friends with a witch who wasn't well.
"It's good to be kind," said Berty's Mum with a hug
as she tucked him in bed and made him feel snug.
"Yes," said Berty. "It made me feel good,
I think that witches are misunderstood!
The witch was kind and in need of a friend;
she looked a lot better in the end."
"Achoo!" went Berty and he started to cough;
he was running a temperature and he felt rather hot.
"Oh dear," said Berty. "I don't feel very well
my nose is blocked up and I can't smell."
"It's ok Berty," replied his mum with a smile,
"I'll take care of you now, at least for a while..."

Printed in the United States
by Baker & Taylor Publisher Services